Sophie's (Friendly) Spiders

Katy Hounsell-Robert

Onwards and Upwards Publishers,

Berkeley House,
11 Nightingale Crescent,
West Horsley,
Surrey,
KT24 6PD,
UK.

www.onwardsandupwards.org

ISBN: 978-1-911086-00-0

Illustrations: Josh Williams

Printed in the UK

Contents

I should like to sincerely thank Mandy Spalding for inspiring and encouraging this book and letting me write about her adventures as a US (then known as USPG) volunteer in Zimbabwe. Also to Revd Jonathan Ford and Mike Potter of Christ Church, Moreton Hall, Bury St Edmunds for their co-operation.

Thanks, too, to Les Underwood of The Arundel Pet Shop, Tansy Standen of Emsworth Aquaria & Reptiles and Simon Williams of Southcoast Exotics & Marines, all of Portsmouth, for their friendly and expert advice on the spider world, also to Tony Penny for sharing his experience of spending a lifetime keeping spiders and snakes in his house, and to Terry Henderson for his help in researching spider life.

Also to Mrs Felicia Munjaidi, Director of Zimbabwe Tourism (London) and Mrs Miriam Panganaya of the Embassy of Zimbabwe (London) for their vivid descriptions of the life and culture in Zim. Also to fellow author Angela McPherson for relating to me her fond experiences of living there as a child and young adult.

Also thanks to David J. Roberts for his careful reading of the early draft and his very helpful comments.

Katy Hounsell-Robert

Foreword

Something for the grown-ups to read!

It may seem strange to write a story about a little girl who turns into a spider and travels to Zimbabwe for the winter mosquito festival, but some years ago I wrote a series of magazine articles about people who had volunteered to go out with USPG[1] to poorer countries to work in orphanages, hospitals and other places needing help. One normally thinks of volunteers as young gap students but these particular volunteers were mature, and academic qualifications were less important than an experience of life and a willingness to get down to whatever needed doing to really help people.

One such volunteer was Mandy Spalding of Bury St Edmunds who gave up a comfortable life to 'do something worthwhile' and live and work in Zimbabwe with children whose parents had died, often from AIDS, and had no one to look after them.

She lived in (sometimes quite dangerous) conditions that most of us would find very hard, but her faith kept her going and also her love for the many children who needed care. However she was very homesick and made friends with some spiders who lived behind photos of her family and friends which she had stuck on the stone wall

---

[1] now called US

of her little hut. She gave them each a name and talked to them.

Around the same time I met a little girl who was terrified of spiders and her mother had to move any spider from a room or passageway where she went. I thought they should both travel to Zimbabwe, albeit for different reasons, in my book 'Sophie's (Friendly) Spiders' and show how fear, prejudice and lack of self-esteem can be overcome (with a bit of 'Outside' help) and also show how brave and selfless these volunteers are and the enormous good they do.

Katy Hounsell-Robert

1

Who's afraid of the big black spider?

'Evening, everyone,' Mike the church youth group leader said cheerfully. 'As usual, let's start our evening with a short prayer.'

And the group of young people ranging from eight to twelve stopped chattering and fooling around, and moved to the chairs at the front of the church, sat down quietly, closed their eyes and lowered their heads.

As Mike began to pray, Sophie's mind began to wander on to what she would buy when she went with Mum to the Christmas market in Bury St Edmunds this Saturday. She loved the Christmas market with the big tree and coloured Christmas lights and the decorated stalls along all the streets and carols and jazz and exciting things to buy you didn't see in the shops. She was hoping to get a new blue collar for Rupert, her dog...

The sound of the word 'Mandy' suddenly made her listen again.

'...And also let us pray for Mandy, our youth helper who is out in Zimbabwe looking after orphaned and abandoned children in the Matthew Rusike Children's Home. Keep her strong and centred. Amen.'

'Amen,' echoed the group in unison.

Mike went on. 'Before we get down to this evening's activities, I just want to remind you about the Christmas Fair in aid of the Children's Home, and if you haven't brought your contributions yet, please bring them to church on Sunday or here next week.'

Grace, one of the older young people, put up her hand, shaking back her long blonde curls that Sophie envied so much. 'Mike, I've brought every book and toy I'm not using anymore,' she boasted. 'They were very expensive too.'

'Good,' nodded Mike. 'I'm sure everyone is giving all they can towards such a good cause.'

Sadie, who was just eight, waved her hand urgently. 'Mike, are we going to buy a pig with the money we make?'

'Well,' said Mike, 'we're going to send the money out to Zimbabwe for them to buy the pig.'

'How much is a pig?' asked Harry, her brother.

'About eighty-five pounds. Now, let's get on with this evening's activity. It's Drama.'

There were great cheers except from some boys who wanted games.

'We're going to divide into three groups of five with team leaders Grace, James and Lee. To make things fair and help you work with different people, I've put folded papers into a hat.' He waved an old battered Victorian top that they used to draw lots. 'Five are marked with H, five with J and five with G. No swapping to be in your friend's team.'

Sophie let the others rush to pick out their papers and then took hers out and opened it. Oh, *fiddle!* – She was in Grace's team. She knew you were all supposed to 'love your neighbour' and all that, but if Grace was a neighbour in the Outer Hebrides, it would suit her better.

The group moved their chairs round noisily to get into the right team and Grace positioned herself grandly in the middle of her five who were mostly much younger than her.

Mike went on. 'I'm going to give you as a theme a well known nursery rhyme and I want you to make up a short play and characters round it. It can be funny or a detective or historic play as all these rhymes are based on things that really happened. We'll perform them this evening and then, if you like, we can put them on again with some dressing up at the Christmas party. Lee's group will do "The Queen of Hearts". Who remembers how it goes?' The whole group laughed and chanted with him while he waved his arms conducting them. 'The Queen of Hearts, she made some tarts, all on a summer's day. The Knave of Hearts, he stole those tarts and took them clean away…' The group finished the rhyme together.

'James's group will do "Humpty Dumpty".'

Again, even louder, the group chanted, 'Humpty Dumpty sat on a wall. Humpty Dumpty had a great fall. Not all the King's horses nor all the King's men could put Humpty Dumpty together again.'

'And Grace's group...' continued Mike. 'Little Miss Muffet sat on a tuffet eating her curds and whey...'

'There came a great spider,' smirked Grace looking at Sophie, 'who sat down beside her and frightened Miss Muffet away.'

Grace *and* spiders! This was even worse. Sophie shivered. Everyone knew how terrified she was of spiders. If she saw one in a passage, someone had to remove it before she would go along it, and if there was one in her bedroom, she screamed until her mother captured it in a pot and threw it out of the window.

'I'm giving you twenty-five minutes to work out your story and rehearse a bit,' went on Mike. 'I'll come round to each group to see how you're getting on. Then we can perform them.'

'Now,' Grace said to her group, 'let's have all your ideas.'

'I vote we make it a detective story,' suggested Chris. 'The curds and whey are poisoned to get rid of Miss Muffet, or something like that.'

'Good, good,' encouraged Grace.

Sophie stayed absolutely silent.

'What are curds and whey?' asked Sadie.

'A sort of yoghurt. Children in the old days ate it,' explained Grace. 'Well, let's choose who will be Miss Muffet and the spider to start with and then we can make up other characters. I think Sadie would be a lovely little Miss Muffet. She's the youngest here and the smallest.'

The rest of the group nodded agreement.

'Then I see Sophie as the spider.'

The group giggled.

'No, no, I don't want to be the spider!' Sophie panicked.

'I think you'd make a lovely big fat spider creeping along behind Miss Muffet. What do the rest of you think?'

'Yes, yes,' they giggled.

Sophie felt more and more distressed. Her chest began to hurt and she felt dizzy and hot.

'*You* be the spider,' she shouted at Grace.

'But you'd make a wonderful spider, wouldn't she, everyone?' Grace smiled forcefully at the other four children who nodded and laughed.

Sophie's fear and horror changed into real fury. She pushed her chair back. 'I have to go to the loo,' she said and went off through the door at the far end of the church while the others carried on planning the story.

All right, she would show everyone. She would really *be* a horrible spider and terrify everyone. How, exactly, she didn't know.

'I want to be the zookeeper,' said Harry. 'I'll come and try and catch the spider, but she gets away.'

'I want to be Miss Muffet's mum,' said Ellie, 'who makes her the curds and whey.'

They were all very engrossed in the story when Mike came to join them and hear their ideas. He noticed that Sophie was not there.

'Do you know where Sophie is, Grace?' he said casually. He always kept an eye on every single child so that no one felt out of it or unhappy.

'I think she's gone to the loo,' said Grace.

Mike moved on to another group to ask if one of them had seen Sophie. Then he heard a terrible scream – as though someone had seen a ghost.

It was Grace. She jumped up, still screaming, pointed in horror at Sophie's chair and ran to the far end of the church.

All three groups immediately turned round to where Grace was pointing and they screamed and ran too and, although this was not really allowed, some scrambled up on to chairs. There was pandemonium.

'What on earth is wrong?' asked Mike and went over closer to see what was causing the panic.

Sophie's chair was completely empty – except for an enormous black spider with red spots glaring at them all.

Sophie's chair was empty except for an enormous black spider.

No one recognises Sophie.

Sophie had no idea what had happened to her. She had been beside herself with fear and anger and then suddenly something clicked inside her and she felt different and unreal, although she was not sure how. Then she felt calmer and so she had come back to sit on her chair.

Why had Grace run to the other end of the church screaming? Why did the rest of the group seem so much bigger and why were they all staring at her in horror or running away screaming? Why did Mike, who also seemed much larger than usual, come over and stand well back to inspect her?

'It's all right,' he said soothingly to the group. 'They don't do any harm but they're a bit scary, aren't they? James and Lee, open the fire door, please.'

The two boys pushed the metal bar down and the heavy door clanged open. At the same time they both kept a wary eye on Sophie as though she was something weird.

'What's wrong?' she tried to say but her throat seemed very tight and she couldn't speak.

Mike took hold of the old Victorian top hat which had held the slips of paper and now seemed enormous, edged towards her and very slowly tried to place it over her. What was he doing? Trying to squash her? Just before the hat crashed down on her, she ran faster than she'd ever run in her life, towards the open fire door, with all the groups still panicking, and out on to the grass. In the chilly air she took some deep breaths and was thinking about going back in, when the fire door was slammed close and locked.

Was it a joke to do with Miss Muffet and the spider? But Mike wouldn't play a joke like that and push her out into the cold. Was the whole thing a dream? No. She really was outside on the cold grass. Sophie decided she might as well go home. She hadn't had time to finish her buttered crumpets for tea and she felt really hungry. She didn't have her coat but she felt quite warm.

The walk to her house was about ten minutes along a narrow footpath with hedges either side and Mandy, who lived a few doors away, always used to come with her and see her safely home. She really missed Mandy. She was like an auntie to her and always round at their house for tea and chat. Now with Mandy away, Mum used to meet her; or Dad, but he was in the Royal Navy and away at sea. She was a bit scared but she thought of the crumpets loaded with butter and started off on the path.

Halfway there she noticed something unusual on top of the hedge on one side. She was a bit short-sighted and there wasn't much light, but this thing was nearly as big as her and dark coloured and had glinting eyes. She'd heard about pet panthers being let loose from homes years ago and they lived free in the countryside. People had seen them. Maybe this was one. Suddenly it parachuted down on to the other side of the hedge and then just as quickly parachuted up back on to the top of the hedge. Then down again. No. It didn't somehow look like a panther. Whatever it was, while it was down the other side of the hedge Sophie decided to move quickly past it towards her home without disturbing it.

Her key was in her bag at the church but Mum would be in and she would ring the bell. However the bell did seem much higher and she had to climb up on the brick wall of the porch, and even then she didn't seem to be able to push very hard. She heard Rupert, her dog, panting at the door as he always did when she came home. Mum came to the door and Sophie walked in expecting her to hug her quickly as she always did, but Mum peered out both ways, looked puzzled and then shut the door. Rupert sniffed Sophie and nuzzled her gently but as though he wasn't quite sure who she was.

Mum went off into the kitchen without speaking and so Sophie went up to her bedroom to put another jersey on. Her arms felt sort of longer and as she was thinking about it she heard people walking along the gravel path and then ringing the bell. She looked out. Mike was standing there with Grace and a policewoman. Mike was holding her bag and coat and looking very serious, and Grace was crying.

Her mother opened the door and stared at the group.

'I'm so sorry, Julie,' said Mike kindly, 'but has Sophie come home?'

'No,' answered Sophie's Mum. 'She's not due yet. I was going to come and meet her in an hour or so. Why?'

'Well, Sophie was in the youth group taking part in the drama activity and then she suddenly disappeared. We looked everywhere that she might be but we couldn't find her,' confessed Mike.

'Nothing to be alarmed about, Mrs Sanders,' the policewoman assured her kindly.

'It's all my fault,' wailed Grace. 'I asked her to be the spider in our play and now she's run away.'

'Oh, Grace, *how could you?* You know she's terrified of spiders,' reproached Mum.

'It was a joke...'

'Do you want to come in and tell me about it?' Mum was now looking very worried.

Mike, Grace and the policewoman came into the house. Sophie decided to let Grace sweat it out a bit and then appear to her mother and tell her she was safe.

The group went into the sitting room leaving the door ajar and Sophie sat on the top of the stairs to listen and see what she could. They all sat down and the policewoman got out a notebook.

'Can you give me a description of Sophie, please, Mrs Sanders?' she asked.

Mum was hardly able to speak but she muttered, 'Yes. She's eleven years old, about four foot ten. She's a bit chubby. She has dark straight hair down to her shoulders and blue eyes...' Then she began to cry.

'She was wearing a red hairband,' added Grace.

'Yes,' went on Mum tearfully, 'I don't know if she was wearing her glasses.'

'I don't think she was wearing her glasses, was she, Grace?' asked Mike.

Grace couldn't remember. Then the policewoman asked for a recent photo and Mum went to a drawer and took one out and gave it to her. Sophie hoped it was the nice photo from last Christmas when she had her hair curled and no glasses and looked quite slim. Still, it was all very exciting, especially as she was quite safe.

'Now, Mrs Sanders, when we've gone, can you look in all the places in the house and garden where Sophie might be hiding and also ring her friends? Often a child hides for some reason and then is ashamed to come out.'

'Yes, of course,' said Mum.

'Thank you, Mrs Sanders – and don't worry,' the policewoman said kindly, 'she can't have gone far. We find missing children usually turn up within a few hours.'

Sophie hid behind the banisters so Mike, Grace and the policewoman didn't see her as they left, and Mum shut the door and went slowly upstairs carrying Sophie's bag and coat. She walked straight past Sophie into her little bedroom and Sophie followed. Mum sat on Sophie's bed and picked up her old teddy bear. She was crying.

'Please let her be safe,' she whispered.

Sophie ran up on to the bed and tried to say, 'Mum, I'm here, I'm safe,' but her throat seemed frozen.

Her mother stared at her and then she took a large empty flower vase from the windowsill and a paper tissue.

'Let's get rid of you,' she muttered, 'before my daughter sees you.' She pushed Sophie into it, opened the window and emptied her out.

Sophie felt something coming out of her body letting her gently down to the ground unharmed. She couldn't believe that her own mother didn't recognise her. *Her own mother didn't recognise her!*

She huddled in the garden for a long time confused and upset. Why was everything suddenly so big and everyone so horrible to her? When the door opened and Rupert came out for his evening exercise, she hurried in, and when he came back and curled up for the night in his basket in the kitchen, she crept in between his big, warm, furry paws and slept there till morning.

Sophie doesn't like what she sees in the mirror.

Sophie woke up suddenly when Rupert got out of his basket and ambled towards the back kitchen door to go out for his early morning exercise. She felt very cold and hoped it had just been a bad dream and everything was back to normal again. Mum, in dressing gown and slippers, was making a cup of tea. Just what Sophie needed. Mum usually took a cup up to her to wake her up and she thought she would save Mum the trouble. She climbed out of Rupert's basket on to the kitchen floor and Mum stared at her.

'You again,' she said not unkindly and brushed her into the little dustpan and threw her out into the garden with Rupert.

Dad had always taught her to think of anything awful happening as a challenge; then to face the challenge and work out how to deal with it. Sophie's present 'challenge' was that she had become something horrid to be got rid of. But she must face it: she must look at herself in a mirror. She edged back into the kitchen and up the stairs into the bathroom where there was a full length mirror. She closed her eyes and then opened them. She saw a large black spider and began to shake with terror. She fearfully put out her right hand and the spider put out its long front leg towards her. Then she saw that the spider was wearing her red hair band round its neck.

'No! No!' she tried to scream but no sound came out. She tried to hit the mirror to break it. Dad's teaching went out of the window. If she really was a spider, she wanted to die. She would go into the woods and wait to die. She was already so hungry she would probably starve to death any minute. She slunk despairingly out of the house and made her way to the woods near the house.

The early morning was chilly but bright and sunny, and she suddenly thought how beautiful the woods were with the green fir trees and golden brown leaves on the ground and the sunlight coming through the bare branches. Then in one of the bare trees she noticed the same creature she had seen yesterday on top of the hedge. It was doing its parachuting down and up as it had done the day before. It was actually brown and its head was quite extraordinary with two very big eyes, four very small eyes below and two medium sized eyes above – and no ears. But it looked kind and, strangely enough, she didn't find it scary and for a while she just stared.

The creature nodded in a friendly way and waved some long legs but kept its distance. Then it called in quite a deep voice, 'Good morning.'

'Good morning,' she answered. She couldn't believe this was happening, especially because her voice seemed to be coming from her legs – and her hearing too.

'I hope you've had breakfast?' it said.

'No,' she answered, 'and I'm very hungry.'

'You won't eat me, will you?' It moved even farther away.

The idea was so disgusting she ignored it.

'I just wanted to make sure. You're bigger than me and big girl spiders often eat smaller boy ones if they're hungry.'

'I'm not a spider,' she told him.

He smiled as if she was joking. 'I was a bit short of bugs last night because of the cold. You won't mind me having a big breakfast, will you? Do excuse me.' He ran after a creature looking like a big ant, caught it in his mouth, squashed it and sucked it like an orange. 'That was good,' he observed, then after a little while he added politely, 'My name is Muffet.'

'I'm Sophie,' she said.

'That's a strange name for a spider,' he replied.

'I'm not a spider,' she repeated firmly. 'I'm a human being.'

'Oh, yes,' he smiled, 'and I'm a kangaroo.' And he leaped after another insect, squashed it and sucked it dry.

'Muffet is a very strange name too,' she observed.

'Oh, almost every eldest boy spider is called Muffet and every eldest girl spider is called Tomasina after Dr Thomas Muffet, the famous scientist who loved spiders and had them all running round his house. He had a daughter – Miss Muffet – but she didn't like spiders.'

'I hate spiders too.'

Muffet laughed, 'But you are a spider.'

Sophie began to cry loudly and could not stop.

'Steady on,' Muffet said. 'You'll frighten all the insects and I won't catch any food.'

But she went on sobbing and sobbing.

'Tell you what,' he said kindly, 'I'm going out to Zimbabwe today or tomorrow for the Festival of Mosquitoes. You can come with me if you like.'

'Zimbabwe?' she repeated still crying. Zimbabwe was where Mandy had gone to work in a children's home but she had no clear idea where it was.

'Yes, the finest mosquitoes are there in the rainy season. Do you want to come?'

Sophie shook her head but stopped crying.

'Look, I have to go and say goodbye to my Mama at Risby Barn before I go,' he said. 'Come with me. She can tell you more about Zimbabwe. This is only my second time.'

Sophie had been with her mum to Risby Barn before. It was only down the road and an amazing place full of beautiful old carpets, furniture, books, glassware, china. But there were no spiders. Mum had checked it out before they went in.

'Quick! There's a van that goes to the barn every Friday morning early,' Muffet said. 'Just by the church. We can go with him.'

He started running very fast. It was amazing how fast you could go with eight legs and Sophie followed him. She should be at school but perhaps Mum had sent a note saying she had disappeared.

The back doors of the van were open while the driver was loading. When he wasn't looking, they climbed in and sat in a corner under a little table with curved legs. Then the driver shut the doors, started the engine and they moved off.

'I was born and brought up in Risby Barn,' Muffet said chewing the remains of another insect he'd picked up on the way. 'Mama lives there in a commune under the thatched roof. It's fun there with plenty to eat but I wanted to lead my own life. It was very educational there. There are books on almost every subject you could want. Mama taught us to read of course and I spent most of my time reading.'

'How did you turn the pages?' Sophie was quite intrigued.

'Two or even one large spider can lift a page at a time. Then you can climb above and hang down on your silk thread. That way you can read a lot at once. Otherwise you have to run across the page and back all the time which is tiring.'

The van stopped and the driver opened the doors and started to unload the boxes.

'We'll get out now,' said Muffet and they ran out straight into Risby Barn. There was not a spider to be seen in the lower part of the barn but as soon as they climbed up into the thatched roof, spiders seemed to be everywhere. Muffet hurried towards a large one that was almost covered by a crowd of tiny spiderlings crawling up her back and round her legs. None of them had ears.

'Mama,' Muffet said, 'I'm going off to Zimbabwe tomorrow. Thought I'd pop in with my friend to say bye-bye and meet the new batch of spiderlings.'

Mama looked vaguely at him.

'I'm Muffet. I was born here two years ago,' he reminded his mother.

'Oh, yes. Of course I recognise you. Oh, help Tomasina catch that beetle. She is so slow. I wonder if she'll ever be able to look after herself.'

'She'll have to learn, won't she, like the rest of us,' replied Muffet taking no notice of Tomasina who was running around madly after a beetle but missing it all the time.

'Muffet's friend, can you catch that beetle for Tomasina? She'll starve if she doesn't catch something soon.'

'I'm not very good…' began Sophie.

'It doesn't matter. I'll do it.' With incredible speed Mama caught a beetle and gave it to Tomasina to suck.

'So you're going on holiday to Zimbabwe? I remember when I was there ages ago. Such happy days. So warm and so many mosquitoes and lovely insects.'

'Can't you go now?' asked Sophie.

'I have too many spiderlings to look after all the time.'

Tomasina had now sucked all her beetle. 'Mama, go Zimbee,' she cooed.

'No, Tomasina. You're too young. You haven't moulted enough and the heat would dry you up. Later your big brother can take you.'

'Muffy, go Zimbee,' shouted Tomasina trying to hook one little leg round Muffet's.

He shook her off. 'It's not Zimbee. It's Zimbabwe. Zim... barb... way.'

'Go barby,' squeaked Tomasina. But Mama lifted her away from Muffet with two of her long legs and gave her another beetle to suck

'Goodbye then, Mama,' said Muffet.

'Goodbye, Muffet's mama,' echoed Sophie.

'Goodbye, goodbye. Enjoy your holiday,' Mama shouted and Muffet pulled out his silk thread and dropped down on to the period costumes, which were soft to land on. Sophie now knew how to pull her silk thread out and followed him.

Outside the barn there were cars parked and a lady carrying plants was opening the boot of her car to put them in. Then she went back to the nursery to get more plants.

'Quick,' said Muffet, 'get in while she's not looking. I know where she's taking the plants in Bury St Edmunds, and it's by the station. From there we can get the train to Cambridge, then King's Cross and then the Tube to Heathrow. Are you coming or not?'

Sophie thought quickly. Not even her mother wanted her. Rupert and the spiders were the only ones who seemed friendly. Going to Zimbabwe for free and seeing where Mandy worked began to seem very attractive. It was a really big step but...

'Yes,' she said determinedly, 'I'll come to Zimbabwe.'

A free trip to Zimbabwe.

When the great train doors slid open, Muffet climbed up and in quickly and turned immediately into the First Class compartment with Sophie following him closely.

'There's more room here and not so many people,' he whispered. 'Get under a seat and stay very still.'

Sophie giggled. It was the first time she'd travelled First Class even if it was under a seat.

Suddenly a woman screamed in another carriage. Sophie was worried that something awful had happened and they would stop the train, and she and Muffet would not get to the airport. Then she heard a little voice calling, 'Muffy, Muffy. Me go Barbee wiv oo.' And Tomasina scuttled in.

'Oh, no!' groaned Muffet. 'How did you get in?'

'Me follow in car and climb in window. Lady cream.'

'Oh, no!' moaned Muffet again. 'You can't come with us. Go back.'

But by now the train was speeding through the countryside.

'She can't jump off now,' objected Sophie. 'It would be dangerous.'

'Then she has to get off at the next stop!'

It took some time before the train stopped again and by then Tomasina had crept into a corner looking dejected and unhappy. 'Tomsina hungee,' she whined.

'You can't push her out without any food,' said Sophie. 'She can't feed herself. What would Mama say?'

'I knew I shouldn't have gone to say goodbye to Mama.' Muffet was very annoyed. 'Spiders are always jumping on you and trying to get rides everywhere.'

They all crouched under the seat with Muffet catching a surprising number of insects and unwillingly giving one every now and again to Tomasina. He was cross with her for following them and cross with Sophie for wanting her to stay.

It was rather boring being on the floor looking at people's shoes and Sophie thought she would climb up on to the top of the seat so she could see the countryside and villages they passed. A ticket collector passed by but didn't notice her and so they arrived safely in Cambridge and ran along to the departure screen to see the train times to London Kings Cross.

A small crowd was looking at it in dismay. All the trains to Kings Cross had been cancelled.

A middle aged man with a look of authority about him, and accompanied by a younger man, called to a station official. 'What's happened? Why are they cancelled?'

'The high winds and rain have derailed some trains. It should be sorted in a couple of hours.'

'That's too late.' The man was very angry. 'I have a plane to catch to Harare in Zimbabwe. Are your people going to fix a bus or something for us?'

The official shook his head apologetically and the man, very angry, picked up his overnight bag and pushed his suitcase out of the station towards the taxis, followed by his companion.

Sophie and Muffet, now carrying Tomasina on his back to speed things up, looked at one another. 'If we can get a lift with him in a taxi, that would be good,' Muffet said, in better temper now, and they followed the two men.

When the taxi driver put the man's suitcase in the boot, they climbed in. It was not a terribly comfortable journey but it went straight to Terminal 4, where the man got out, the boot was opened and the suitcase and the spiders came out.

'This is where we transfer to his overnight bag,' said Muffet. 'We don't want to go in the freezing hold under the plane. Jump into that open pocket on his bag.' So still carrying Tomasina, he and Sophie jumped in.

In the pocket there was a bottle of water with some drips running down the side and they had a drink. Sophie was so relieved that now she could suck up water like a spider.

. 'If we can get a lift with him in a taxi, that would be good,'
Muffet said.

In the bag compartment they sailed unnoticed through check-in and passport control. Then the water bottle was thrown away and Muffet instructed them to get out of the bag as it went through the x-ray security check. They climbed up the wall and along the ceiling and then let themselves down on their silk threads into the bag again and were carried on to the plane. Luckily they were in Business Class with more space to move around.

It was going to be a very long journey. Tomasina was tired and cross and wanted to sleep. She asked for a bedtime story.

'Mama has so spoilt her,' Muffet complained but he began telling her, 'Once upon a time there was a lady called Arachne who spun the finest, strongest silk thread and wove the most beautiful pieces of tapestry anywhere. Athene, the goddess of wisdom and crafts, heard about her and came to see her work. So what do you think happened?'

'Don't know,' whispered Tomasina.

'The goddess was so impressed with Arachne's weaving, she decided to honour her so that Arachne would be able to weave beautiful, beautiful tapestries all the time for ever and ever. So what did she do?'

'Don't know,' whispered Tomasina again.

'She changed her into a spider who of course weaves more beautifully than anyone in the world.'

'I think that's wrong,' objected Sophie politely. 'The story is that Arachne was arrogant and boasted that she could weave better than the goddess and so the goddess challenged Arachne to a weaving competition. The goddess won it, but then as punishment for Arachne claiming to be better than her she condemned her to be a spider.'

Muffet seemed not to hear and went on with his story. 'Of course this was a long time ago but we are Arachne's thousands times thousands great-grandchildren. No more stories now. Go to sleep.'

'More tory,' shouted Tomasina getting very upset.

'I can tell you a story,' said Sophie.

'Only if it's nice about spiders. We only tell spiderlings inspiring stories to help them love themselves,' warned Muffet.

'This is about King Bruce, where a spider helps a human being.'

Muffet nodded. 'All right.'

'Many years ago there was a Scottish King called Bruce,' Sophie told her. 'He was fighting the English King. He lost a battle but escaped and hid from the English in a cave. He was very depressed and thought he would never beat the English again. Then he saw a spider climbing the wall. She got so far and fell back, but she tried again and got so far and then fell back. He watched fascinated. Then after many tries she actually climbed to the top... "If she can do this, so can I," said Bruce. He collected his men and challenged the English again – and *won*.'

Sophie could see that both Tomasina and Muffet were asleep, and she was very tired too. But it sounded from the announcement as though they were landing – not in Harare in Zimbabwe, though, but in Johannesburg where they would transfer on to another plane for

Harare. So she curled up in her corner and stayed awake, keeping guard.

The bag was lifted and then after a while carried on to another plane. When it had taken off and was flying smoothly through the air, she thought she would climb out of the bag and look around for any food she could eat. The two men were dozing but on their meal tray Sophie saw some large cakes which were probably biscuit crumbs. She tried to suck some up but it wasn't easy and she choked.

The elderly man suddenly opened his eyes and he and Sophie stared at one another. She thought he would try to kill her and she was starting to run, when he smiled. 'Hello, little spider,' he said. 'I've not seen one like you before.' He nudged his younger companion who also woke up. 'George, look at this beautiful specimen. Can you identify it?'

The companion peered at Sophie. 'Unless it got on at Jo'burg, it can't be a black widow. Could be a false one? I've seen them with very different red designs on the body. This one is much larger than usual and I've never seen the red band round the neck before.'

'Just think, George, we may have discovered a new family of black widow. But be careful. They can give a nasty bite.' He pressed the bell above him and a stewardess came along immediately.

'My dear,' he said charmingly. 'Could you please get me a largish bottle with a lid to put this lovely creature in?'

She jumped back in terror but then composed herself and forced a smile. 'Yes, of course, sir,' she said calmly and went off very quickly.

In a few seconds a steward arrived. 'I do apologise, sir,' he said. 'We're shortly landing in Harare. We shall have the whole place fumigated so that all insects are destroyed.'

'No, no, don't do that. Please. This is a rare specimen. I'm an entomologist – that is, I research and teach about insects – and I specialise in arachnology – that is, spiders. I'd like to keep this specimen safe to observe it.'

Sophie decided very quickly that it was safer to run back into the bag compartment where Muffet was now awake and seemed more switched on about what to do. Then the landing notice went up and everyone got into position and clicked their seatbelts.

The elderly man looked around for Sophie everywhere except in his bag, and very shortly they all arrived in Harare, the capital city of Zimbabwe.

Meeting Mandy's spiders.

As soon as the elderly man and his companion left the plane, Muffet said, 'Out!' and they climbed out of the bag, let themselves down on their silk threads and ran across the hot red ground out of the airport. Very different from London Heathrow. The smell too was like diesel oil mixed with hot dust and sweet flower fragrances.

'Now, we need to get down to the south,' Muffet said. 'The festival is really great there. You cannot imagine how big and juicy the mosquitoes are.' He was licking his lips at the idea.

But Sophie had seen a signpost to Harare city saying 20 km and a small one to Epworth saying 10 km. She remembered this was where Mandy was. 'Oh, Muffet, let's go and see Mandy first. She's in Epworth,' she said excitedly.

'What or who is Mandy?'

'She's a great friend of my family. When she was depressed and wanted to do something worthwhile in her life, our vicar, Rev'd Jonathan Ford, suggested she came out to Zimbabwe to work in a children's home in Epworth. I'd love to see her.'

Muffet looked decidedly unwilling.

'I can't come all the way to Zimbabwe and not see her,' insisted Sophie.

'Tomsina want Mandy,' whined Tomasina. 'Tomsina hungee.'

'Mandy is not something to eat,' Muffet told Tomasina crossly and then turned to Sophie equally crossly. 'I should never have invited you to come to Zimbabwe.' Then because he was tired and didn't really feel like more travelling straight away, he gave in. 'All right, just a couple of days. The question now is how do we *get* to Epworth? But first let's have a drink.'

He and Tomasina ran to the nearest pothole full of rain water and drank and drank. Sophie followed more slowly. She was thirsty, and drinking from drips on a sterilised water bottle in the plane was one thing but drinking from street water...

Cars and small coaches had picked up the passengers from the plane and now there didn't seem to be any form of transport around. There were some brown spiders sitting in the sun on a large rock and Muffet approached them but keeping his distance. Yes, they knew the children's home but it was quite a way.

'If the wind is in the right direction, you can parachute on your silk thread,' said one. 'But there's not much wind today after the rains. Your best bet is to jump into the big basket of that Weya woman sitting on the grass feeding her baby. In a minute she'll be walking to

Epworth with handmade goods to sell there. Keep well down. There are a lot of nasty birds hovering around who love eating spiders.'

The woman didn't notice them climbing into the basket which was full of bags, skirts and scarves all sewn with coloured beads, and when she had fed the baby and put him on her back, she lifted the basket up on to her head and began walking slowly and rhythmically along the road, avoiding potholes. It was quite enjoyable being carried along looking at the countryside, sometimes passing fields where women were labouring and sometimes beautiful purple Jacaranda trees and green shrubs, although much of the land was bare, red and muddy with big pools of water. The baby whimpered a bit and Sophie swung down on her thread and up again to amuse him. He gurgled delightedly, and if she stopped, he cried. After a while they passed broken down wooden dwellings and roadside stalls and soon came to a high concrete fence with barbed wire along the top enclosing a collection of one-storey buildings. As they got nearer, Sophie read:

Matthew Rusike Children's Home

Sophie had no idea what time of day it was, but as the sun was directly overhead it must be about midday. Rather unwillingly she said goodbye to the baby, and the spiders let themselves down on their silk threads and walked through the open gate where a lot of children's clothes were drying on lines and some barefoot children were playing games on the bare ground and others under the shade of a tree.

At the same time that the spiders entered, a small truck covered in red dust drove in and a lady who looked as if she was in charge got out and opened the door for two children to get out. One was a boy about four and the other a girl about three or less. They were very dirty and barefoot, their clothes were old and the little girl was crying. The lady kindly took them by the hand and called for Mandy.

Then, to Sophie's delight, Mandy came out of a building, looking just the same as she had in Bury St Edmunds. Maybe a bit slimmer and her short hair a bit blonder in the sun, but she had her big glasses she always wore and looked very cheerful. Sophie ran up to say, 'Mandy, we're here.' But Mandy hurried straight over to the lady and bent down and hugged each child warmly.

The lady said, 'This is Tendai and his little sister, Nyasha. Their parents died of AIDS and their grandma has been looking after them, but now she's in hospital. Perhaps you can sort them out.'

'Yes, of course, Matron,' Mandy answered and hugged the children again. 'Welcome to our big family, Tendai and Nyasha. We're just having our lunch so you've come at the right time.'

'Lunch...' sighed Sophie. She was still so hungry but she knew that human food was too big for her. Yet she still couldn't face the idea of scrunching insects and sucking the juice.

Matron went off leaving Mandy to take the children into a building, and the spiders followed. It was the dining room and small children were sitting at the table eating hungrily.

'Great,' said Muffet. 'Where there's food, there's insects and usually water.'

Carrying Tomasina, he made his way to the rubbish bins where insects including mosquitoes were hovering, but Sophie followed Mandy and the children. Mandy sat them down and put a plate of food in front of them which looked like maize porridge and vegetables, and then got them each a cup of water from the tap. She got herself the same meal.

'I hope you like sadza and vegetables,' she said, 'because we have it every day.'

'We *only* have sadza and vegetables,' Tendai explained between devouring large mouthfuls of food.

'The good news is that at the weekend the supermarket gives us all the leftovers and so we have a feast. The children here love cake soaked in gravy.'

'Lovely!' said Nyasha excitedly. 'Grandma sometimes gave us chicken – but not very often. Is Grandma going to be all right?'

'Well,' Mandy said kindly, 'she is ill at the moment but you can stay here as long as you like.'

When they had eaten all they could and cheered up, a lady in a bright top and skirt patterned with big flowers came along. 'This is my colleague Nyasha, the same name as you,' Mandy told the little girl. 'She's going to show you both where you can sleep and give you some new clothes.' She hugged the children again and they went off happily with grown-up Nyasha.

By then Muffet had caught a lot of insects round the waste bin and given some to Tomasina, and Sophie had picked up some bits of sadza which she managed to rinse down with water, and so they were fairly content and when Mandy left, they followed her across the bare red ground to a row of small huts, where she went into one.

The walls and floor were stone and the single bed with a thin mattress was made of iron. There was a small table, a chair, an electric ring, a small wall mirror, and stuck on the walls were photos of Bury St Edmunds and Mandy's family and friends. Sophie ran up on to the table followed by Muffet and Tomasina. 'Mandy, it's so good to see you again,' she said.

Mandy stared at them and smiled. 'Hello, new spiders,' she said. 'Have you come to join my spider guys? They live behind my photos. Let me introduce you.' She went to a photo of the youth group which Sophie recognised had been taken before Mandy had left to come to Zimbabwe. 'This is the youth group at my church in Bury St Edmunds. They're a great group and write every week, and they're raising money to buy us a pig.'

She pulled the corner slightly away from the wall and a very large spider appeared. It was very different from Muffet being golden brown coloured with a black violin shape on the back of its head. The eyes were different too with two big ones in the centre and a pair of smaller ones either side.

'This is the youth group at my church in Bury St Edmunds,'
Mandy said.

'This is Mutsa,' Mandy said and as two smaller spiders appeared with the same marking, 'These are Chipo and Fadzai, her daughters.' Then pointing at a rather battered sheet web in a corner of the ceiling, 'This is where Precious lives on her own in her web.'

Precious, a small, wispy, grey spider came out and went back quickly. Mandy then pulled a photo of her pet cat away from the wall and three spiders smaller than the others came out. 'These are Tongai, Tinotenda and Innocent. I think they're brothers.'

'Oh, dear,' grumbled Muffet. 'I'm a wolf spider and they're all violin spiders except Precious. I foresee fighting!'

The seven resident spiders regarded the visitors with hostility.

'We've been here since Mandy came. It's our territory,' Mutsa said rudely.

'We appreciate that,' Muffet answered nervously. 'We're actually on our way down south for the mosquito festival.'

'What are you waiting for then?' growled Mutsa.

But Tongai told them, 'The festival starts tonight here too,' and the brothers jigged about giggling.

Sophie suddenly realised that she was bigger than Mutsa and so she took a good breath and announced, 'Mandy is my mother's friend, and mine. We've known her in England and as she has welcomed us we're going to stay… for a little while anyway.'

Mutsa glared and went back behind the photo.

Mandy of course did not hear the conversation and smiled at them all. 'Got to go to work,' she told them. 'See you later this evening.'

While she was away, Precious was busy making repairs to her web to catch mosquitoes and the others rested ready for the event.

Night fell. Mandy was in her bed under the mosquito net fast asleep. Every spider was poised ready to attack and in the early hours of the morning there was a loud, high-pitched whine. The mosquitoes had arrived.

The mosquitoes are bitten before they bite.

Sophie had never experienced anything like this in her life. She had been bitten by one or two mosquitoes in the garden but here hundreds seemed to suddenly be inside the room in the dark, like a great whirring cloud.

Over the high, loud whine, Mutsa, who reminded Sophie more and more of Grace, shouted that residents must have first choice of mosquitoes, as she and the other violin spiders pounced on the creatures – sometimes missing but more often catching. Precious calmly sat in her web and when a mosquito landed on the sticky strands and stuck fast, she rushed down, wrapped it in her silk and took it back to kill and eat. Then she was back for another one.

The whining went on ceaselessly as more and more mosquitoes arrived apparently from nowhere and the hungry spiders caught and scrunched them, drinking their juice and dropping the remains on the floor. Sophie could just about see in the dim light and was so fascinated she forgot to be horrified. Tomasina jumped around delightedly trying to catch a mosquito but they were too quick for her and Muffet had to give her some.

'Why do they all come inside?' Sophie asked Muffet.

'Because,' he answered, 'mother mosquitoes need blood to give themselves enough protein to feed their children. When they smell human bodies lying asleep uncovered, they come in swarms because human flesh is easy to bite into.'

Sophie didn't know this but even so she didn't like them any more because of it.

'But they carry diseases like malaria and things,' she said. 'Aren't you worried you'll catch something?'

'No,' answered Muffet. 'Spiders only catch insects! Why don't you try and catch one? Mosquitoes jump up and back to get away so you have to be above and behind them... like *this*,' and he expertly snatched a mosquito from the air and scrunched it. Sophie told herself she would have to get used to eating raw insects but somehow not yet. She half-heartedly tried to copy Muffet but didn't do any better than Tomasina.

Suddenly heavy rain began to fall. It poured endlessly through the holes in the roof, ran under the door and through the gaps in the window frame. The invasion of mosquitoes slowly stopped but instead, little frogs began to come in, croaking and hopping around.

'Oh, no! Frogs! Take cover or they'll eat us,' Mutsa yelled.

Precious stayed in her web while the others ran up on to the table where they were safe. By then they had all eaten enough – too much in fact – and intoxicated with the excitement and the mosquito juice, the two different types of spiders gave up the idea of fighting and started celebrating the festival in song and dance while keeping an eye on the frogs. Precious strummed on her web like a harp and sang out of tune. The brothers let down their silk threads and went up and down performing acrobatic tricks, and the sisters performed a sort of ballet dance moving gracefully with their eight legs. Mutsa stretched a silk sheet tightly across a hole in the table and with four legs drummed on it.

'Come on,' the brothers called to Muffet. 'What can *you* do?'

'Well, let me think,' Muffet pondered slowly and then he looked around for some small scraps of paper and rolled eight of them into balls, sealing them with his silk. He began conjuring with six legs while two stayed on the ground. He went faster and faster and faster. Everyone clapped and then they all turned to Sophie. It was her turn.

'I can't do anything,' she said.

'She can. She tell tories about King Boos,' stated Tomasina.

'What's a king boos?' asked Chipo

'It's a human thing. It's a leader – someone who tells everyone what to do,' Mutsa informed her.

'Good tory. About pider who helps hooman,' Tomasina informed them.

'Let's have it then,' said Mutsa and everyone sat and listened attentively and clapped. Sophie felt very pleased. She didn't usually do anything where people clapped her.

Mutsa sat down with Sophie and became very philosophic. 'As you know, we encourage baby spiderlings to become independent and stand on their eight feet from the beginning. Each of us has to be responsible for our own lives.'

Sophie nodded in agreement.

'We are *all* very lucky that Mandy is happy to let us stay here,' Mutsa went on. 'Most humans like to control other creatures and take away their independence. If they can eat them or their produce, they imprison them on farms. They imprison others for sport or to be their pet servants like dogs.'

Sophie thought about Rupert and how they kept him in the house and trained him to do things – but only in a nice way.

'Humans will never be able to do that with spiders,' said Mutsa firmly. 'That's why they don't like us.'

'For example,' Mutsa continued, 'our silk is very fine and soft but stronger than the same thickness of steel. They tried to put us in silk farms like those poor, stupid silk worms to make silk endlessly for them. But we had ways of not letting them use us.'

'How?'

'Very simple. As you know, we spiders fight one another a lot and eat one another, and so when a lot of spiders were put together in one cage, you can imagine what happened.'

'They ate one another?'

Mutsa nodded gleefully. 'Humans would never admit that they learn from spiders. For example, humans learned how to spin, how to weave cloth by watching spiders.'

Sophie nodded. 'Yes, probably.'

'Without a doubt. Then there is the World Wide Web. Humans got the idea from our webs but they got themselves stuck on to their own webs and everyone else's and can't get away. Just like an insect on a spider's web.'

Sophie thought this was pretty true except Mum wouldn't let her be on the Internet more than an hour every day – unless it was research for school – and two at the weekend.

'And they have never ever shown any gratitude to us for eating the millions of insects who would eat their crops or bother them,' added Mutsa.

Sophie did feel a bit ashamed about this.

'I hope you don't mind me saying this,' said Mutsa, 'but it is strange for you not to eat insects.'

'I think it's horrible,' said Sophie.

'And you seem to have a good relationship with humans. Do you know many?'

'Well, yes,' Sophie laughed. 'My parents are humans and I'm human, really, but at the moment I'm a spider.'

'You are a very unusual looking spider,' Mutsa observed almost reverently. 'There is a goddess who is also a spider and a human. Are you she?'

'Oh, no, no, nothing like that,' protested Sophie. She went to the photo of the youth group that included her and Mandy, which seemed enormous of course. 'Look, that's Mandy. And that's me as a human. And the others are the youth group.'

Mutsa was deeply impressed and obviously believed that Sophie was definitely an undercover goddess.

The rain suddenly stopped. The sun was rising. Mandy's alarm went and she got up and went off with a wash bag. Then she came back and got dressed. By this time all the resident spiders were asleep.

'I'm off to morning prayer, breakfast and work,' Mandy told them. 'Be back later. Don't fight.'

'I don't think I want to hang around here. That Mutsa might get more aggressive this morning and one of them might eat Tomasina,' said Muffet. 'It would be safer for us to move on.'

'Oh, no, let's stay a bit longer,' Sophie begged.

Tomasina was unusually quiet and said nothing.

'All right, just one more night,' agreed Muffet.

'Let's go and find Mandy in the dining room then,' suggested Sophie. 'She'll look after us and we can see what the children are doing.'

Muffet nodded and as Tomasina seemed almost asleep he carried her on his back and they went to spend the day with Mandy.

7

It is hard work at the children's home.

The early morning sky was so beautiful with the golden sun radiating into pink and blue streams of light, making even the squat one-storey buildings look quite ethereal. Although every block looked the same, Sophie remembered the way to the dining room where Mandy and the rest of the staff were at prayers. They said the 'Our Father' prayer in Shona which fascinated Sophie but Muffet wasn't interested in prayers and took Tomasina over to the kitchen bin for insects.

She watched in amazement as Nyasha put milk, sugar, tea bags and hot water all together into a pot and stirred. All the staff drank it and seemed to enjoy it. A stream of older children came in their school uniforms to have a bowl of milky sadza and the special tea and then went off, and then the under fives came to have their breakfast. This took a lot longer as there were a number under eighteen months and Mandy and the other staff had to feed them. Little Nyasha, dressed now in a pretty cotton dress, and Tendai, in cotton T-shirt and shorts, seemed quite happy now and devoured the sadza porridge and chatted with other children. Sophie counted around one hundred and twenty children who had breakfast altogether, from babies to sixteen-year-old youths.

Mandy, Nyasha and another lady in a long, loose, bright, flowered dress went out of the dining room. Sophie followed them and Muffet unwillingly left the kitchen bin and, still grimly carrying Tomasina on his back, followed her. The three staff went into another block with big sinks, big buckets underneath and ironing boards where there were stacks of clothes to be washed and piles of clothes to be ironed.

Nyasha turned a tap on and a drip of water came out. Mandy also turned another tap on and no water came out at all. They all looked at one another and turned the taps off.

'Maybe the water will be on in a couple of hours,' Nyasha said hopefully.

'Let's get on with the ironing anyway,' suggested Mandy. 'The mosquito eggs need to be killed before they hatch.'

Everyone agreed and started on the enormous pile of ironing. Nyasha started singing a jolly rhythmic song in Shona. The others joined in heartily and Sophie really enjoyed it although she didn't understand a word. She felt so sorry for Mandy who was used to an up-to-date washing machine and tumble dryer at home. It must be awful to have to wash so many clothes and sheets and towels by hand like a hundred years ago. What a relief the water was off.

'This is boring,' muttered Muffet. 'I think we ought to start moving down to the south.'

'Just a bit longer,' said Sophie. 'Then I can tell everyone at home what it's like here.'

Then she realised she couldn't because she was a spider.

After two hours Nyasha made more tea and Matron came to share it with them sitting outside under a tree.

'Matron, I'd like to go into Harare to send an e-mail,' Mandy said. 'We can't do the washing till the water comes on and I could pick up the post at the same time.'

'Yes, of course,' Matron agreed. 'Take the truck with you.'

'Thank you, Matron.' Mandy looked very relieved.

She left the others and made her way to the small dusty truck followed by the three spiders. Muffet looked more cheerful. 'If we go into Harare,' he said, 'maybe I can find a train or bus to go down south.'

'Tomsina no train,' moaned Tomasina. 'Hot. Go sleep.'

'You'll have to come with me or those violin spiders might eat you,' Muffet retorted.

'It's definitely a good idea to find out about transport in Harare,' said Sophie soothingly.

Mandy noticed the spiders sitting in the back of the truck. 'Hello again,' she said. 'Are you coming with me? It's a very bumpy ride, I'm afraid. But at least it's better than the bus.'

As she pulled out into the road, the truck almost immediately went down into a very deep pothole and if the spiders had not had sticky pads on their feet, they would have been thrown to the other side of the truck.

After a mile or so they passed two young children who looked like twins, waiting by a small pole on the other side of the road.

'That's the bus stop going the other way,' Mandy said. 'Poor little things. The buses are so overcrowded, you can't always get on and you arrive like a damp rag.'

It was very exciting and different, Sophie thought, to pass all the wayside stalls with handmade rugs, pots, fruits and different foods as they tried not to be too thrown about. Mandy drove into the city, which had more squat buildings and also very high ones, and the women were wearing bright-coloured dresses, some carrying goods on their heads. It was all so exotic with so much movement and African music playing. Mandy parked in a cool square with trees and went to get out.

'If you want to come with me,' she told the spiders, 'you had better sit on the rim of my hat.' She took it off so they could run on to it. Sophie did but Muffet decided to stay in the cool under a tree with Tomasina who seemed completely knocked out.

Mandy pushed her way through a narrow, hot street into a small Internet cafe where several people were at computers. She sat down, took her hat off and Sophie ran round so she could watch the screen. Mandy typed in her password and began her e-mail.

'If you want to come with me,' Mandy told the spiders,
'you had better sit on the rim of my hat.'

Mike,

As always, thank you so much for your e-mails and prayers. They are the only thing that's kept me going as well as my own prayers. I know I always seem cheerful and positive but I'm not really that inside.

She paused and took her glasses off to wipe tears welling up in her eyes and running down her cheeks. She wiped her glasses and dried her eyes, then went on typing.

It was like a miracle for Jonathan to suggest I came here, for this chance to actually do something worthwhile with my life, and for you and the youth group to help me with my fare and give so much support. But I'm not sure I can really go on.

The first couple of weeks when I stayed at the college it seemed like a holiday but now it's terribly hot all the time and heavy, and when it rains, it pours and comes through holes in my roof and everything gets soaked.

There's mosquitoes and frogs – I had a frog in my bag yesterday.

The showers are totally open. Everyone goes together naked.

We have to collect water in buckets all the time as reserve and if it runs out, you can imagine what it's like in the toilets.

Then the electricity goes off and the girls have to cook outside on fire pits.

I shouldn't complain. The children never do. They're lovely. Some of their stories are tragic. The mother of two children murdered their father and then died in prison, and they were put out on the street. Now I have to say they've settled in and seem very happy.

Sorry about this. I just pray I can stick it out. I know I can come home any time but I don't want to let everyone down – or myself.

You know what? The sadza and veg is really boring every meal so I'm going to the supermarket to buy something exciting and have a little party in my own stone hut. With my spiders.

Love to you all,

Mandy xxx

Mandy wiped her eyes again and paid the Internet man, then left with Sophie back on her hat. Sophie was dumbfounded and horrified. She had never seen Mandy like this and there are some grown-ups like teachers and leaders you never expect to cry. If Mandy couldn't cope and came back to Bury St Edmunds, what would they do about the pig?

Mandy put on her cheerful face again and went through more crowded, noisy streets that were fascinating for Sophie seated safely in the rim of the hat. The next stop was the post office where Mandy waited in a queue and signed for the post. Then, all done, she went into a little supermarket and asked the assistant for something tasty that she could cook.

'Caterpillars are very tasty with tomatoes and seasoning,' suggested the assistant and so Mandy bought a small packet of dried ones.

Back in the cool square, Muffet and Tomasina joined them in the truck. Muffet had found out that he could either fly or go by train down to Bulawayo and was quite pleased. Tomasina was very quiet.

As Mandy drove back slowly towards the children's home, the two twins were still waiting at the bus stop. Mandy stopped. 'The buses are not very frequent,' she called. 'Can I give you a lift? Where are you going?'

The boy said, half in English with some Shona words, 'Nowhere. Our mother left us here.'

'Right,' said Mandy, 'get in and I'll take you to our Home.'

The girl went to jump in and then saw the spiders and screamed.

'It's all right. They're my friends,' Mandy assured her. 'They won't hurt you.'

She nodded but kept her distance as she got in. The boy hobbled slowly and seemed to have painful feet.

'Is there something wrong with your feet?' asked Mandy.

'Our mother burned the soles of my feet so I would not run home,' he said.

'We'll sort that out for you,' Mandy told him kindly. She lifted him up into the truck and drove everyone back home.

Spiders and humans have challenges to face.

As soon as they got back into Mandy's room, Tomasina fell off Muffet's back and collapsed in a little screwed up ball on the stone floor.

'Water... Mama...' she gasped.

'Is she all right?' Sophie asked. 'Is it the heat?' Then she noticed the skin on Tomasina's legs cracking. 'Look at her skin!' she cried in horror.

'I think she's moulting,' said Muffet. 'Mama said she hadn't moulted enough. Oh, why did I go to say goodbye to Mama? If I hadn't, this wouldn't have happened over here.'

The seven resident spiders gradually emerged from behind their photos and watched sympathetically.

'Moulting is awful,' said Chipo to her sister. 'Do you remember when we last moulted? We felt awful for days.'

Fadzai nodded.

Suddenly Precious, who rarely showed much interest in what the other spiders were doing, came out on her web. 'I'll look after her,' she announced firmly. 'She needs quiet and not to be disturbed. She can stay with me on my web until her new skin hardens.'

Muffet looked very relieved when Precious came down on her silk thread and carried Tomasina up. 'I just hope Precious doesn't feel like eating her while her skin is soft,' he commented.

The other spiders discussed together all the symptoms they had when they moulted and how many times they had moulted.

Mutsa observed, 'She'll be all right. It's a natural thing, even if some spiderlings don't survive.' Then, noticing Sophie looking very worried, she sat down with her in a respectful way. 'Generally, only a few don't make it. I don't think even human-lings always survive.'

'No,' agreed Sophie. 'In the old days many human children died as babies or in their first few years. But now it's rare for a baby not to survive.'

Mandy, unaware of the moulting, came in triumphantly waving a letter. 'Spider guys, my youth group have written to me. I'm going to cook my caterpillars and read my letter while it's still light and the electricity is on.'

She emptied the packet of dried caterpillars into a saucepan of water and turned on the electric ring. Soon a very unpleasant smell wafted around. The resident spiders retreated behind the photos, and Sophie and Muffet moved to the open door where the air was coming in.

Mandy read aloud excitedly.

Dear Mandy,

We hope you are OK and not being bitten all over by mosquitoes.

We have to tell you something awful has happened.

Sophie moved a bit nearer to hear what it was.

Sophie has disappeared and the police have been searching everywhere and dredging ponds. And it's all in the papers with her photo. Sophie's mum is trying hard to be cheerful and goes to work every day and comes to church but she is so worried, and Sophie's dad has come home on compassionate leave.

What happened was that one evening we were doing Drama, and Grace asked her to be a spider and she disappeared.

We are praying for her at church and school and at the youth group. Please pray for her there too.

Another awful thing is that we collected a lot of things to be sold at the Christmas Fair to give to you to buy a pig for the children's home. They were in cardboard boxes but someone left a door open when it was pouring with rain and a lot of the things got so wet they can't be sold. But don't worry. We'll try and do something else.

Love from us all and longing to see you again,

Grace, Lee, James, Sadie, Harry, Matilda,
Katy, Oscar, Isabel, Josh, Amy,
Sam, William, Ellie, Alex, Rachel,
George, Tamsin and Mike.

X X X X X X X

Mandy read the letter again and again. 'Poor little Sophie and Sophie's mum and dad. How awful! ... Oh, spider guys, here I am moaning about my life and this poor little girl is missing.'

The spiders now switched their sympathy to the human crisis but there was nothing they could do to help any more than Mandy could help with the moulting. Sophie, on the other hand, tried not to show how really chuffed she was that so much fuss was being made about her.

'Spider guys, we must pray for her that she will be safe,' said Mandy and knelt down on the stone floor to say a prayer. The spiders were not into prayers but they kept quiet. Sophie put her two front legs together although she thought it was quite funny praying for herself to be safe when she was sitting right in front of Mandy. But of course her mum and dad and everyone were terribly worried and although her mother hadn't recognised her, Sophie loved her and didn't want her to be so upset.

Mandy suddenly said she was going to turn the boiling caterpillars off and see if she could phone Sophie's parents. Sophie was going to scuttle after her but she also wanted to stay to see Tomasina moulting. The moulting won.

It seemed really weird. All the skin on Tomasina's body was lifting off and she could see Tomasina's new body, exactly the same as the old one, only bigger and like jelly. Then slowly the old skin came off and lay like a body mask. It was a bit like when Sophie cut her knee and it formed a scab; when the new skin grew underneath, it pushed the scab off.

'The best thing now, Tomasina,' said Precious comfortingly, 'is to hang down on your silk thread to let your skin harden. Then nothing will touch you. I'll keep you safe.'

Tomasina nodded. She still seemed very quiet.

The spiders got on with resting or activities, and later in the evening Mandy came back. 'The phone lines were down,' she told them. 'No one can phone or e-mail.' She sniffed the air. 'What is that dreadful smell?' she wondered.

That night they all got ready again for the mosquito festival but as well as heavy rain there was lightning and thunder, so loud and near that Sophie was a bit frightened. The mosquito invasion was disappointing and the celebration not so lively. Precious didn't want to strum on her web as it would disturb Tomasina, Chipo and Fadzai sang lullabies to Tomasina to keep her happy, and Mutsa kept on cheering everyone up by talking about spiderlings who had not made it through the moulting.

In the morning the sun rose brilliantly, Precious's web sparkled in the sunlight, and Tomasina seemed a bright new spiderling and able to speak more clearly. 'I am a big spiderling now,' she said triumphantly. 'I can catch my own mosquitoes and scrunch them up.'

'Thank goodness for that,' muttered Muffet.

'But you must stay hanging on your thread for another day or so,' Precious told her.

'When your skin is completely hardened, we must make tracks down to the south,' Muffet said.

'No,' replied Tomasina. 'I'm going to stay with my new mama. I like it here.'

Muffet looked very relieved.

Mandy, still unaware of this great spider event, seemed very sad and worried about Sophie, but put on her cheerful face as she went off to work.

Sophie decided to stay and watch Tomasina finish moulting. She suddenly had a great interest in making a web. Although Muffet and Tomasina were wolf spiders and ran after their prey to catch them, if she was to stay a spider she rather fancied making a pretty web to sit and wait in for an insect to stick on it.

'Could you show me how to make a web?' she asked Precious.

'It's very easy,' Precious explained. 'You just pull out your silk thread and hang it on to a corner of a wall, and go backwards and forwards to make a mesh. I made this one ages ago and I only do repairs to it now.'

'Can you show me how to make one of those big round webs?'

Precious seemed quite offended. 'My spider group doesn't make that type of web. We manage to catch plenty of insects on this sheet web.'

'Yes, it *is* a very lovely design,' Sophie agreed.

'Well, it's not *that* lovely but it's practical – and what is a web for except to catch insects and live in? If spiders want to go round showing off how artistic they are, that's their lookout.'

'Quite so,' answered Sophie.

After a long pause Precious said rather unwillingly, 'But if you want to learn how to make that type of web, everyone is going to church tomorrow and then on a Christmas picnic out in the country. You'll see plenty of trees and you would probably come across the Epeiridae spider. That is the only species that makes the big round web. They are not very beautiful and so they compensate by making something beautiful.'

'Wow!' thought Sophie. 'A Christmas picnic out in the country!' And she forgot all about everyone worrying about her.

Church and the Christmas picnic.

The sunset was particularly beautiful that evening, although Mandy commented that there was a wind rising and she hoped the weather would be fine for the picnic. It was also a good night for mosquitoes and as Muffet no longer had to nanny Tomasina, he caught some for Sophie, scrunching them up first so she could just drink the juice. By now Sophie was grateful for anything and the flavour was not too bad.

Mandy was obviously still very concerned about Sophie's disappearance and all night Sophie was trying to think what she could do to help her. When Mandy went off to the showers, she noticed that her pocket Bible was on her bedside table as Mandy read from it every day, and it occurred to Sophie that she might find a psalm that would lift Mandy's spirits. She thought of 'The Lord is my Shepherd' which everyone knew and was very comforting.

'Spider guys,' she said, 'wake up! We've got to do a bit of lifting. Not you, Tomasina, but everyone else.'

There were grunts from behind the photos, moaning that they were shattered from eating too many mosquitoes.

'It's important,' insisted Sophie. 'It's to help Mandy.'

'Out, everyone!' ordered Mutsa.

Slowly they all crawled out yawning.

'Muffet, you told me that you can read a book by several spiders lifting and turning a page over.'

Muffet nodded. 'But how will us reading a book help Mandy?'

'We find Psalm 23 for *her* to read,' Sophie told them. 'The words will lift her spirits.'

'Yes, do as she says,' ordered Mutsa. 'She is a very wise spider.' She winked knowingly at Sophie.

'Psalms is in the middle of the Bible,' said Sophie. 'So we need to open it in the centre.'

Muffet worked out that if they slid something very thin but strong like a knife into the middle of the Bible, all the spiders could squeeze in, place their weight against the top half and push the book open. Then they could find the page and lift it the same way. He noticed a long nail file which would not be too heavy, and on a 'one, two, three' from Mutsa they lifted it on three sides, gently inserted the end into the middle of the Bible, and started to push.

'Oh, I'm being squashed,' yelled Chipo.

They stopped while she moved out and then pushed further in. Then they all sat on top of the protruding end and bounced. The Bible opened. The five younger spiders cheered.

Muffet swung up above the open pages. 'We are into Psalms but we are at Psalm 18 so we need to lift and turn *that* way.' He pointed to the back of the book.

They all pushed the file in and lifted again.

Muffet read:

𝔐𝔶 𝔊𝔬𝔡, 𝔪𝔶 𝔊𝔬𝔡, 𝔴𝔥𝔶 𝔥𝔞𝔰𝔱 𝔱𝔥𝔬𝔲 𝔣𝔬𝔯𝔰𝔞𝔨𝔢𝔫 𝔪𝔢 𝔞𝔫𝔡 𝔴𝔥𝔶 𝔞𝔯𝔱 𝔱𝔥𝔬𝔲 𝔰𝔬 𝔣𝔞𝔯 𝔣𝔯𝔬𝔪 𝔥𝔢𝔩𝔭𝔦𝔫𝔤 𝔪𝔢?

'Oh no!' cried Sophie. 'Is that Psalm 23?'

'Sorry, no,' said Muffet. 'That's 22. 23 is here on the same page.'

𝔗𝔥𝔢 𝔏𝔬𝔯𝔡 𝔦𝔰 𝔪𝔶 𝔰𝔥𝔢𝔭𝔥𝔢𝔯𝔡. 𝔍 𝔰𝔥𝔞𝔩𝔩 𝔫𝔬𝔱 𝔴𝔞𝔫𝔱. 𝔥𝔢 𝔪𝔞𝔨𝔢𝔱𝔥 𝔪𝔢 𝔱𝔬 𝔩𝔦𝔢 𝔡𝔬𝔴𝔫 𝔦𝔫 𝔤𝔯𝔢𝔢𝔫 𝔭𝔞𝔰𝔱𝔲𝔯𝔢𝔰. 𝔥𝔢 𝔩𝔢𝔞𝔡𝔢𝔱𝔥 𝔪𝔢 𝔟𝔢𝔰𝔦𝔡𝔢 𝔱𝔥𝔢 𝔰𝔱𝔦𝔩𝔩 𝔴𝔞𝔱𝔢𝔯𝔰.

'That's very nice,' said Mutsa.

Mandy came back, dressed in a long, pretty patterned cotton dress and then noticed the open Bible. To make sure she read it, Sophie and Muffet went up and down on their threads landing each time on Psalm 23. Mandy read it quietly, smiled and said a short, silent prayer. Then she announced she was going to church and on a picnic, if any spider wanted to come. Only Sophie seemed to want to come and when she saw her hovering, she put down her hat so Sophie could run on to the rim.

In the main entrance over a hundred excited children were there – the girls in pretty, colourful dresses and the boys in clean T-shirts and shorts – and both men and women staff were dressed smartly, some in traditional rich-coloured clothes. One member of staff, who was staying with the children who were not well, came to see the party off. Meanwhile Matron ushered the children, chattering and bouncing, along the road with all the people living in the rundown shacks along the roadside coming out to look at them and wish them well. The little boy with the burnt feet was being carried on the shoulders of Lloyd, a young, strong local volunteer, and seemed recovered from the day before.

It took nearly fifteen minutes to walk to the church, a small brick building with a gable roof, already packed out with people all in their Sunday best. Was Sophie glad she could sit on Mandy's hat and not be squashed!

The service began. A lot of people danced to the hymns which were sung in Shona but to well known tunes, but it was so hot that after a little while Matron nodded at Mandy and Nyasha and they brought the younger children out to sit under a tree.

'Now,' Matron said to the group, 'I'm going to tell you all a Christmas story. It's a bit different but it's about all of you.'

The children sat on the grass and listened attentively.

Matron fanned herself as she spoke. 'Once upon a time, not so long ago, there was a man who wanted to serve God and preach and convert people, but as he went about he was saddened to see many little children and older ones too who were on the street with no money, no home and no education.'

'Education is very important, isn't it, Matron?' said little Nyasha.

'It is, Nyasha,' agreed Matron.

'Why were there so many children like that, Matron?' asked Tendai.

'Our country was very poor and often families couldn't afford to feed the children. Then often parents died and there was no one to look after the orphans. So this man, this minister, took as many children as he could squeeze into his house, and he and his wife fed them, looked after them and taught them some lessons. But then he found many more homeless children he just couldn't take in, so he asked for help and money to build more houses and have more people to help him. This is where you are all at home now – because of the love and kindness of this good man and his wife. You all know his name.'

'Matthew Rusike,' they all shouted.

'Yes. You all belong to Matthew Rusike's family and you all have one birthday together on...'

'January 2nd,' they yelled.

By now the people were coming out of church and a red bus drove up and parked outside. Inside were several staff with huge boxes of food, plastic pots and bottles of drink.

'The bus company has kindly let us have a bus for the day driven by their best driver,' Matron told everyone. 'So we're going on a Christmas picnic which the local supermarkets and shops and our friends have given us to enjoy.'

It was not a very big bus but some of the little ones sat on the older ones' knees and everyone seemed to squeeze in. As they drove along, a pleasant breeze kept them cool. Sophie was very happy hiding in the brim of Mandy's hat and was enjoying herself, seeing the beautiful countryside.

The driver drove as smoothly as he could, as the roads were not that even, and into the Chinoyi National Park where they all went into the caves and saw the underground pools. It was so beautiful. Sophie thought she would love to come back as a human, to see it all again. Then the staff carried the boxes and pots from the bus on to a grassy area with shading trees, gave each child a paper plate and plastic cup, and then started dishing out cold rice, potatoes, pieces of chicken and gravy, and pouring out fizzy lemonade. The children were so happy and when they had eaten, they started to play games in groups, some quietly in the cool and others chasing one another round the shrubs.

Sophie wandered off looking for a tree with a spider's web and found one hanging from a branch. She climbed up and came face to face with its weaver who, as Precious had said, was rather a strange shape.

'I like your web very much,' she said politely.

The spider ignored her.

'Could you show me how to make a web like that?' she asked.

'No. I just do it without thinking,' it said.

'Could you make another one so I could watch?'

'Not now. It takes nearly an hour to make.'

'Oh,' said Sophie very disappointed.

'My neighbour had hers torn by a bird and she is going to make a new one any moment,' the spider said helpfully. 'She's just there. Go and watch her.'

The neighbour took no notice of Sophie crouching down to watch her. First she attached her silk thread to a nob on the branch, and then she walked round to find another nob to secure it and make a sort of tight washing line. Next she made a parallel slack thread under the 'washing line' and then from the centre of the slack thread she dropped straight down on her thread and fixed the end to a rock on the ground. Now trailing her silken thread she scampered up and down the threads already there to make a shape with spokes like a bicycle wheel. She was so fast and accurate, Sophie was amazed.

'How do you put on the sticky stuff to catch insects?' she asked politely.

The neighbour said nothing but began weaving a new shining thread through the spokes. That must be the sticky thread.

Sophie was going to ask if she could have a go but she heard Matron calling everyone and she had to go back.

On the way home most of the younger children slept soundly but Sophie loved looking out and really hoped she would return one day and see more of Zimbabwe.

Back home the children sleepily got out of the bus, thanked the driver gratefully and went to their dormitories. Some of the staff went with the little ones to help.

'Mandy,' called Matron, 'there's a phone call for you. It's urgent, from Mike, and I think it's good news.'

Mandy ran to the phone. 'Perhaps they've found Sophie,' she said.

Sophie knew that couldn't have happened and so she scuttled after Mandy to hear what the good news was.

Buying a pig can be dangerous.

Mandy picked up the phone excitedly. 'Hello, Mike. Is it news of Sophie?' she asked.

'Sadly no,' Sophie heard Mike's voice come over loud and clear. 'But we are praying of course and the search is still on. Sophie's dad did an appeal on local TV which we hope will have some effect. No, the good news is that we have collected the money for a pig – and not just one pig but *two*. It was a combination of talents from the youth group and Sophie's dad. I think they told you about the sale items getting wet...'

'Yes, I knew about that,' said Mandy.

'Well, as spiders seem to be connected with Sophie's disappearance – or maybe not – Grace, whom we know can be a pain but is also very bright, came up with the idea of making a big spider's web made of rope for people to try to walk on without falling off. It's not that easy! Sophie's dad got a pile of thick old rope and spliced it into a web shape. People paid twenty-five pence, and if they got to the centre without falling off, they were given cakes. If they fell off, three of the youth group dressed as spiders came out and dabbed them with flour and water. I have to say I fell off a lot of times.'

'That does sound fun,' laughed Mandy. 'I'm glad *I* didn't have to do it!'

'Yes, it was good fun and everyone enjoyed watching it and taking part. Then the youth group auctioned the remaining cakes and we made over two hundred pounds. I've already transferred it through to your bank in Harare and you can withdraw what you need tomorrow.'

'Brilliant!' said Mandy. 'At least *some* news is good. Thanks so much.'

'The group did ask for one favour. Could one of the pigs be named *Hope* – short for "Hear Our Prayer Every day"?'

'I can't see that being a problem,' Mandy agreed.

'How are you now?' asked Mike.

'Better, thank you. Must learn to face challenges with joy.'

In the morning Mandy was up earlier than usual and very excited. 'I'm off to the bank in Harare,' she told the spiders who were mostly half asleep except for Sophie. 'Then I'm going on to a little farmstead to get the two pigs. Do any of you spider guys want to come?'

Sophie ran forward and Muffet and Mutsa also followed. Tomasina was still hanging on her thread drying out but when she showed interest, Precious shook her head. 'You're not ready,' she told Tomasina. 'You could be damaged.'

'We certainly don't want that,' muttered Muffet.

Chipo and Fadzai preferred to stay with Tomasina entertaining her, and the brothers were too tired after their lively night, so Mandy and the three spiders went to get into the truck. There was great excitement at the entrance. The children had decorated the new pigpen with flowers and were getting garlands ready to hang round the necks of the pigs. Supervised by Matron, they crowded round to watch Nyasha and Lloyd, the local volunteer, get into the truck with Mandy.

'When you get the cash,' Matron advised them, 'each one of you take a third and put it into something that doesn't look as if it would contain money, like a carrier bag with fruit in it. If people see you coming out of a bank, they could follow you and mug you, but this way it divides the risk. It's a pity the farmer doesn't have a bank account but many don't.'

'When we come back,' Mandy told the children, 'we shall have two lovely young pigs with us. They'll produce lots of lovely piglets and we can sell them and make money to buy a lot of things we need here.'

'Don't stay away longer than you have to,' said Matron. 'I hear that a wind is rising and you don't want to get blown off the road.'

'I should think we three plus two heavy pigs will hold the truck down,' laughed Mandy.

The children all cheered as Mandy drove out, carefully avoiding the nearest pothole.

Nyasha and Lloyd didn't bother too much about having three spiders in the back of the truck but Muffet kept a good distance from Mutsa. She was still suspect.

Into Harare they went and parked in the little square but this time all the spiders went with the humans and sat on Mandy's broad-brimmed hat. Mandy led everyone along a main street and into a modern smart bank where Nyasha and Lloyd sat on comfortable chairs while she waited in a long queue and then spoke to a counter assistant. After twenty minutes she was given a very large pack of notes which she divided between Nyasha, Lloyd and herself.

Lloyd knew the area and the farm they were going to, and back in the truck he started giving directions. Soon they were out in the country on very bad roads. They passed fields under water, mud huts, broken down sheds but also areas with masses of avocados and mangoes growing in the sun and trees where bright-coloured birds were flying about. They turned off the road into one that was not much more than a mud track with two strips of tarmac to drive along, but Mandy drove well and slowly and everyone was in good spirits and singing popular Shona songs. Then another truck appeared behind them and followed, keeping at a short distance.

'Someone else is coming to buy a pig,' observed Nyasha.

The truck moved closer and they could see three men in it looking quite well dressed and pleasant. It came nearer and nearer until it was on Mandy's tail.

'Do we know these people?' she asked.

Suddenly it curved past them going through a water-logged ditch and then took up position in front of Mandy, blocking her path. She had to stop. The men were waving as though they needed to tell Mandy something.

'Has anything dropped off our truck?' she asked the others.

While the older driver stayed in the truck, the other two in smart jeans and dark T-shirts got out. Suddenly the older of these two whipped out a small black gun and pointed it at them. Mandy, Nyasha and Lloyd sat frozen in their truck, totally terrified, as were the spiders.

The gunman indicated for them to get out of the truck and the other man, who was not much more than a teenager, opened the truck door on Lloyd's side. Lloyd resisted and the teenager pulled him out roughly. Lloyd then spoke in Shona to them saying they were from the Matthew Rusike Children's Home and had no money or arms. The two women were good people working there to help abandoned children. He asked them to let the women go, if not him.

'We're in this together, Lloyd,' muttered Mandy firmly. 'Whatever they do, they do to all of us.'

Nyasha nodded her head vigorously. She was too terrified to speak.

The gunman snorted and indicated he wanted them all to get out and lie face down with arms outstretched in front of their truck. The teenager then pushed Lloyd on to the ground down in front of the gunman and went round to open the driver's door. He pulled Mandy out so roughly that her hat was knocked on to the seat, and he threw her to the ground face down. Then he did the same to Nyasha while all the time the gunman had his gun trained on all three. He noticed Nyasha clutching her bag of fruit very possessively and told the teenager to take it. He emptied out the contents including the wad of notes and put them into his bag.

'Go along with it, everyone,' whispered Mandy tensely in English. 'It's only money. Just pray!'

Meanwhile the spiders, also quite shocked, were crouching in the back wondering how they could help.

'Most people, even big, brave men, are frightened of spiders,' whispered Mutsa. Let's jump on the man with the gun.'

'And pray like anything!' said Sophie.

So together the three spiders jumped out and ran towards the gunman who only noticed them when they were climbing up his legs. He yelled, terrified, and let forth a stream of abuse in Shona while trying to brush them off.

Then the gun went off.

The three spiders jumped out and ran towards the gunman.

11

A high price to pay for two pigs.

Everyone was shocked and terrified. Mandy, Nyasha and Lloyd lying face down in the mud hardly dared move in case they were shot while the gunman danced around trying to get rid of the spiders who clung on like mad. He managed to shake Muffet off momentarily but then the spider parachuted back. The three humans prayed aloud and the teenager, caught between removing the spiders that were aggravating the gunman and robbing the humans, kicked them and told them in Shona to 'shut up'.

'Pray! Pray like mad!' shouted Sophie. 'We need a miracle.'

'But you're a spider goddess,' yelled Mutsa. 'Can't *you* perform a miracle?'

'No,' cried Sophie. 'Pray to Almighty God.'

Suddenly the wind Matron had warned them about, which had been slowly rising, began to blow much harder. The gunman jumping about in a frenzy tripped on the root of the nearby Baobab tree and nearly fell over. The gun went off again.

Disturbed by the loud gunshots and the fierce wind, tarantulas who had been sheltering inside the tree came out, thinking they were under attack. An angry regiment of brown hairy baboon tarantulas ran towards the gunman.

The gunman fired at them but that incensed them more and they kept on relentlessly, quickly reaching his shoes. The driver started up the engine, the teenager dropped the bag with the money and jumped into the truck, and the gunman, still holding the gun, ran to join them. Both the driver and teenager shouted at the gunman angrily as though blaming him. Sophie, Mutsa and Muffet jumped off him to safety as he leaped into the truck, which speeded off along the track, churning up mud everywhere.

Suddenly it was very quiet. The tarantulas looked around for the enemy and slowly realised it had disappeared. But then, to Sophie's horror, they focused on Mutsa, Muffet and her, who would be a nice tasty meal for them.

'Spider guys, run for it!' she yelled. And they ran for dear life into Mandy's truck and hid under her hat.

Muffet ran more slowly as he had lost a leg in the fight with the gunman. 'It doesn't matter,' he told Sophie. 'Another one will grow again in a little while.'

The tarantulas seemed not to notice the prostrate humans and ambled back to their shelter. Mandy, Nyasha and Lloyd slowly picked themselves up and gazed at one another. Their faces and the front of their clothes were covered in red mud. They began laughing and hugging one another, thanking God and the spiders and the wind for saving them.

'What were they shouting at the gunman, Lloyd?' Mandy asked.

'They were saying the spiders were his fault; that his neighbour had got the witchdoctor to put a curse on him because he'd stolen a cooking pot from her.'

'Oh, dear!' commented Mandy. 'How far is the farm now, Lloyd?'

'Only a few hundred metres.'

'Then let's go on and do what we set out to do before we were so rudely interrupted,' she suggested, trying to brush the mud off her hands.

Still badly shaken, they got into the truck again. Mandy picked up her hat and laughed to see the spiders hiding there.

'Good idea of yours,' she said. 'Now you can sit on top of my hat.'

She took a deep breath and started the engine. Nyasha started singing, 'Praise the Lord!' and everyone joined in.

When they arrived and got out of the truck, the farmer came out to greet them and stared unbelievingly at their faces and clothes covered in red mud.

'We don't always look like this,' joked Mandy. 'We had a bit of a tussle with a gunman who wanted to take the money.'

'Oh, yes,' the farmer replied. 'My cousin had her bag snatched last week. The man who robbed her looked perfectly normal and friendly and then suddenly grabbed it and ran. Come and sit down and have some mango juice, and my wife can help clean you up.'

The spiders also got out and wandered over to the pigpen. There were some older, big fat pigs and some small piglets in a large enclosure, but in another small one were two young, very attractive, slim pigs.

'I've never seen a pig before,' observed Mutsa. 'Let's have a ride on them.'

When Mandy and her colleagues, looking a lot cleaner than before, came out to see the two pigs, the spiders were happily jumping from the back of one to the other's and enjoying themselves enormously.

'Are these our pigs?' asked Mandy. 'Aren't they beautiful!'

The pigs came up to greet the humans thinking they would get some food.

'They're a very friendly couple of sisters,' the farmer said. 'Are you happy with them?'

Lloyd knew more about swine than the others. He examined them and agreed they were a fine couple of Mukota pigs. The money was handed over and the truck brought near the pen, opened up and the ramp put down for the pigs to walk up.

'It would be safer if you had a closed truck,' the farmer said, 'but I don't think they will be able to jump out. They've never travelled in a truck before and so they won't do anything while you're moving.'

So off they all went again, singing and in good spirits but this time with two happy pigs.

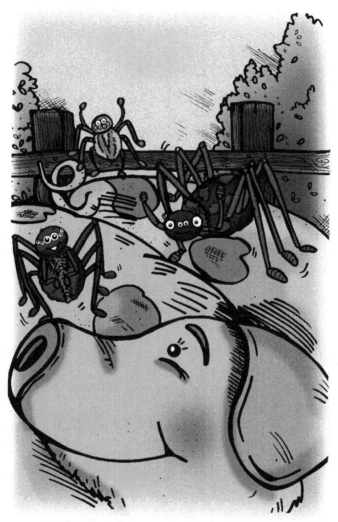

The spiders were happily jumping from the back of one pig to the other's and enjoying themselves enormously.

The journey back seemed much shorter as they didn't have to go into Harare, and as they approached the children's home, they slowed down as some of the children and staff had come out to greet them, cheering and clapping.

One of the pigs began to get agitated and she suddenly jumped out of the truck on to the road and started running across a field. Mandy stopped and Nyasha, Lloyd and some of the children ran after her. The pig was very fast but Lloyd and Nyasha ran ahead of her to try to cut her off while the children ran either side of her, and so in the end she had to turn back and was shooed into the children's home.

The children had made little flags with pigs drawn on them, which they waved while they sang. As Mandy drove the truck with the other pig in and let her out down the ramp into the new clean enclosure, her sister was pushed in with her and the children leaned over and threw garlands over their necks.

'Everyone,' announced Mandy, 'we must thank the young people in Bury St Edmunds for these two lovely pigs. They have asked for one to be called Hope. Are you happy with this?'

'Oh, yes,' they all said. 'Hope is nice.'

'What does Hope mean?' asked one child in Shona.

'It's Tariro,' said another.

'How about calling them Hope and Tariro then?' suggested Matron.

There were great cheers for Hope and Tariro, and Mutsa jumped on to Hope's back while Muffet and

Sophie jumped on to Tariro's. Sophie was a bit sad that none of the humans had realised that they had helped get rid of the robbers but the most important thing was that all the money was saved and the lovely pigs were here.

12

The end of the adventure.

Muffet now decided he was going down to Bulawayo in the south to enjoy the mosquito festival there.

'Will you be able to manage, though, with a leg missing?' asked Sophie sympathetically.

'Oh, yes,' he replied. 'I've known spiders to lose at least four legs and still run like mad. Anyway, it will grow perfectly well after the next moult.'

'But why go down all that way when there are loads of mosquitoes here?'

'Well, to tell you the truth, last year I met a very nice wolf spider like myself down there. She was very young then, but now maybe we can be friends...' He looked a bit coy.

'But what about Chipo and Fadzai? They're nice young spiders,' teased Sophie.

'We only mate with our own type of spider. They are okay but they're violin spiders.'

Sophie thought to herself that he was not going to want herself or Tomasina hanging around when he was courting in Bulawayo. Tomasina had already chosen to stay with Precious but what was *she* going to do? Here Mandy protected her and she was accepted by the other spiders and Mutsa still treated her as though she was some sort of spider goddess, but perhaps they might not always be so benign. Mandy would go back home after a while and she would be left on her own. Suddenly she thought of home, her bedroom and her teddy bear, and Mum and Dad and Rupert, and the church youth group, and Mike – and even Grace. She really missed them.

'Do you think I could get back to Bury St Edmunds?' she asked Muffet.

'Of course,' he said. 'I'm going to get a flight to Bulawayo so I can go with you to the airport and make sure you go Business Class on the right plane.'

But then, Sophie told herself, she would still be a spider. She thought how she and the other spiders had been friends with Mandy when she was lonely and then stopped the robbers taking the money. Perhaps she could do other things to help people in a spidery way. Perhaps she could make beautiful webs in the garden which would glisten in the morning dew – except she still hadn't learned properly how to do it.

'If you want me to go with you to the airport, you'll have to go tomorrow,' Muffet reminded her. 'That's when I'm going.'

Tomorrow! That was very soon. She wanted to say goodbye to all the spiders and the humans she had made friends with. But she was really longing to be home too.

'Tomorrow then,' she assented.

That night there was a bumper invasion of mosquitoes, and all the spiders toasted her health and Muffet's and wished them well and a good journey. Tomasina seemed only mildly sad to see her big brother go.

Early in the morning they picked up a lift from a man on a bicycle who was so sleepy he didn't really notice them sitting on the top of his rear mudguard.

They arrived at the airport and Muffet spotted a lady with an overnight bag at the Business Class desk. He told Sophie to climb into the open side pocket. It was soft leather and comfortable but the lady's scent was a bit strong. It was quite sad to say goodbye to Muffet.

'Maybe we'll meet again,' she said.

'Probably not, but it's been good to know you,' he replied and hurried off on his seven legs.

Then as she ran along the ceiling to avoid going under the security x-ray machine, she suddenly saw the elderly entomologist going through on his own. He had been very kind and even if he wanted to put her in a bottle, he would look after her and feed her and only observe her and she would be safe. So when he was picking up his bag, she crept into it. This time he noticed her and smiled.

'Hello, young lady,' he said. 'Are you going back to the UK as well?'

She found herself answering in a human voice. It was rather hoarse from not using it for a while but it was definitely human. 'Yes, I'm going back to Bury St Edmunds,' she answered.

The entomologist stared in amazement and looked around for a ventriloquist of some sort.

'I am really a girl, actually, but somehow turned into a spider,' Sophie laughed.

The entomologist nodded as if it was the most natural thing in the world.

On the flight she sat on his tray and they talked together about spiders and her stay in Zimbabwe. The steward thought he heard two people talking where the entomologist was sitting but he could only see the elderly man.

'I'll look after you and make sure you get on the train from Cambridge to Bury. Perhaps we could meet later and you can tell me more about the secret life of spiders. What an experience! How lucky you are!'

Sophie thought that she would really prefer to be a girl than a talking spider.

That evening, still a few days before Christmas, Sophie's parents had a phone call from the policewoman. She said, 'We have found a young girl fitting the description of your daughter wandering around Bury St Edmunds station. She seemed a bit dazed and had no coat or bag, but we have taken her to the police station and given her some tea and made sure she's not hurt. Can you come and see if she is your Sophie?'

Their reunion was tearful and emotional. Sophie was so glad to be back with Mum, Dad and Rupert again that she almost forgot about being in Zimbabwe with the spiders.

Mum kept on asking, 'Where have you been? What happened? Are you all right?'

And Sophie kept on saying, 'Yes, I'm fine. It was fine. Everyone was very kind.'

Mike and the youth group were so excited, they kept on hugging her and wanting to be with her. They were just about to perform the nursery rhyme plays at the Christmas party and Sophie asked if she could still play the spider in the Miss Muffet play.

'Yes, of course, Sophie,' said Grace, almost in awe at the incredible change in her.

Sophie played the part so realistically, scrunching imaginary insects and being quiet and friendly while Miss Muffet was screaming her head off, that she received loud, enthusiastic applause.

Despite everyone trying to find out where Sophie had been and what she had done, Sophie remained silent. She thought a great deal about the adventure in Zimbabwe, and at Easter when she and some of the youth group were going to be confirmed, she asked Mike and the vicar if she could make a confession of faith in the church to the people attending the confirmation. Mike was pleased to see how dedicated and confident she had become.

Her parents were coming to the event of course and also Mandy, who had come home on holiday with the great news that Hope and Tariro had each produced nine beautiful piglets, to be sold to help pay for a better water system.

Sophie stood up on the altar dais appearing tall and confident with her dark hair curled and a red head band holding it back. 'I was very afraid,' she said clearly, 'of something I did not understand. I saw only a dark patch of fear and hate. Then a hand came and forced me into the dark patch and it seemed to just dissolve into friendly, pure light.'

Then she looked directly at Mandy. 'I am also ashamed that I looked down on orphaned children in a poor country with pity, for it is they who should pity us. They have the real wealth: gratitude, humility and love, which shapes them into fine people. Many of us are selfish, spoilt and demanding but we can change. God's divine wisdom is everywhere, even if we have to travel across the world to be made aware of it.'

Later she remembered she had not learned properly to make a big sparkling spider's web, but perhaps it was enough for her to appreciate and value this unique masterpiece of art and design as part of God's creation.

Recommended Reading

Ben's Bees

Katy Hounsell-Robert

Ben is excited to spend the summer holidays helping Gramps to look after his bees and collect their honey. But when he and his cousin Martha mysteriously turn into bees themselves, they must quickly learn the rules of the hive community. They soon discover that their new bee friends are in great danger as a young, selfish Queen seeks to establish her rule over the colony.

The Secret of Sizeville

Andrew Phillips

In Sizeville everything and everyone is either very tall or very small. It is a town with a big secret, but a tiny boy soon uncovers it...

Andrew Phillips

Available from

www.onwardsandupwards.org